**Please check all items for damages
before leaving the Library.
Thereafter you will be held
responsible for all injuries
to items beyond reasonable wear.**

Helen M. Plum Memorial Library

Lombard, Illinois

A daily fine will be charged for
overdue materials.

NOV 2013

CORNERSTONES OF FREEDOM™

THE GETTYSBURG ADDRESS

BY JOSH GREGORY

CHILDREN'S PRESS®
An Imprint of Scholastic Inc.
New York Toronto London Auckland Sydney
Mexico City New Delhi Hong Kong
Danbury, Connecticut

BRINGING HISTORY to LIFE

Content Consultant
James Marten, PhD
Professor and Chair, History Department
Marquette University
Milwaukee, Wisconsin

Library of Congress Cataloging-in-Publication Data

Gregory, Josh.
   The Gettysburg address / by Josh Gregory.
      pages cm.—(Cornerstones of freedom)
   Includes bibliographical references and index.
   ISBN 978-0-531-28204-5 (lib. bdg.) — ISBN 978-0-531-27669-3 (pbk.)
   1. Lincoln, Abraham, 1809–1865. Gettysburg address—Juvenile literature.
   2. United States—History—Civil War, 1861–1865—Juvenile literature. I.
   Title.
   E475.55.G74 2013
   973.7'349—dc23   2013000078

SCHOLASTIC, CHILDREN'S PRESS, CORNERSTONES OF FREEDOM™,
and associated logos are trademarks and/or registered trademarks of
Scholastic Inc.

1 2 3 4 5 6 7 8 9 10 R 23 22 21 20 19 18 17 16 15 14

Photographs © 2014: Alamy Images: 37 (Archive Farms. Inc.), 19, 57 top
(Pictorial Press Ltd); AP Images: 33 (Carolyn Kaster), 14, 15, 16, 29, 55, 59
(North Wind Picture Archives), 5 bottom, 17, 20, 36, 46; Architect of the
Capitol: 7; Art Resource/The New York Public Library: 26; Bridgeman Art
Library/David Bachrach/Private Collection: 34; Corbis Images: 4 top, 4
bottom, 10, 12, 38, 43, 51, 58 (Bettmann), 22, 27; Getty Images: back cover
(Gene Chutka), 40 (George Eastman House), 25, 47 (Kean Collection), 44
(Library of Congress), cover (Stock Montage); Library of Congress: 11,
24, 56 (Alexander Gardner), 32 (Brady National Photographic Art Gallery,
Washington DC), 30 (Brady's National Photographic Portrait Galleries),
31 (Currier & Ives), 5 top, 50 (John Hay Papers/Manuscript Division), 42
(Matthew B. Brady), 2, 3, 41 (Sherwood Lithograph Co.), 39 (William B.
Momberger), 49; National Geographic Stock/Tom Lovell: 54; The Granger
Collection: 6, 8; Courtesy of the House Divided Project at Dickinson
College: 28, 57 bottom; Thinkstock/iStockphoto: 48.

Did you know that studying history can be fun?

BRING HISTORY TO LIFE by becoming a history investigator. Examine the evidence (primary and secondary source materials); cross-examine the people and witnesses. Take a look at what was happening at the time—but be careful! What happened years ago might suddenly become incredibly interesting and change the way you think!

Contents

4

A New Union

At the Battles of Lexington and Concord, 95 American colonists and 273 British soldiers were killed.

In the spring of 1775, shots were fired in the small British colony of Massachusetts. The resulting battle kicked off a war that pitted Massachusetts and its 12 sister colonies against the ruling government of Great Britain.

As the war progressed, representatives from each of the 13 colonies formed the Continental Congress to discuss their goals. Debates lasted for more than a year. Southern plantation owners clashed with northern merchants and businessmen, each trying to protect their own interests. Despite their differences, the Congress managed to reach a decision. A committee was chosen to write a formal letter to the British king George III declaring independence, and committee member Thomas Jefferson wrote the first **draft**. After a series of edits to the document, the Continental Congress adopted the Declaration of Independence on July 4, 1776, with **unanimous** approval.

For the remainder of the war, the colonies were united in the fight for independence. Even at the war's end, the former colonies chose to stay together under a single government, the United States of America. However, as the country grew and changed, regional differences in **economy** and culture would threaten to tear apart the Union less than a century later.

Only 12 of the 13 colonies approved the Declaration of Independence. New York did not participate in the vote.

WAS SIGNED BY 56 REPRESENTATIVES.

CHAPTER I

SPLIT IN TWO

Slaves were forced to spend long hours performing backbreaking labor without receiving any sort of payment.

IN THE 19TH CENTURY, Northern and Southern states grew further apart. The South's plantation economy depended on slave labor for producing vast fields of crops. The North's economy was based more on **industries**, which employed workers and had little need for slavery. Northern states began outlawing the increasingly unpopular institution of slavery. As the country expanded westward, the argument over allowing slavery in these new territories deepened the separation between the North and South. Many Southerners began to believe that slavery—and therefore their economy—was threatened. By the mid-1800s, some began calling for their states to **secede**. They hoped to form a new nation that would protect slavery and the Southern plantation economy.

Abraham Lincoln and Stephen A. Douglas debated each other seven times during the 1858 Senate race, with each debate lasting for three hours.

A New Leader

In 1858, a little-known politician from Illinois named Abraham Lincoln decided to run against Congressman Stephen A. Douglas for a seat in the U.S. Senate. The two engaged in a series of long debates. One of the topics they discussed was slavery. At the time, neither candidate was completely for or against slavery. In 1854, Douglas had supported a law that would let settlers in the territories of Kansas and Nebraska choose whether or not to allow slavery. Lincoln, however, believed that slavery should simply not be allowed in the territories. He didn't want the terrible practice to spread as the country continued growing westward.

Lincoln also believed strongly that slavery could not exist alongside states where it was illegal. In one famous speech, given when he accepted the Republican Party's nomination to run for the Illinois Senate, Lincoln said, "A house divided against itself cannot stand. I believe this government cannot endure, permanently, half slave and half free."

People across the nation watched as Lincoln and Douglas debated each other, turning Lincoln into a nationally known political figure. Lincoln's persuasive speeches and well-reasoned debate responses quickly won over many of the people who heard him speak or read his words in newspapers.

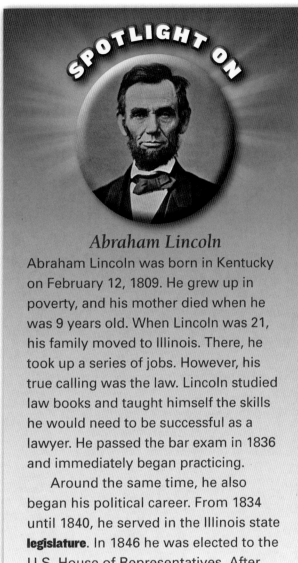

SPOTLIGHT ON

Abraham Lincoln

Abraham Lincoln was born in Kentucky on February 12, 1809. He grew up in poverty, and his mother died when he was 9 years old. When Lincoln was 21, his family moved to Illinois. There, he took up a series of jobs. However, his true calling was the law. Lincoln studied law books and taught himself the skills he would need to be successful as a lawyer. He passed the bar exam in 1836 and immediately began practicing.

Around the same time, he also began his political career. From 1834 until 1840, he served in the Illinois state **legislature**. In 1846 he was elected to the U.S. House of Representatives. After his term ended in 1849, he took a break from politics for several years before challenging Stephen Douglas for the U.S. Senate seat in 1858.

Though Lincoln lost the 1858 Senate election, his campaign gave him the support he needed to seek an even higher office. Two years later, he began campaigning for president.

The House Divides

While Lincoln based his presidential campaign on keeping the nation united, the states continued to divide. When the November 6, 1860, election arrived, Lincoln lost in every Southern state. In some states, his name didn't even appear on the ballot. Many Southerners believed he would lead the nation toward **abolition**, despite his promise not to do so. However, he secured enough votes in the rest of the country to win the election.

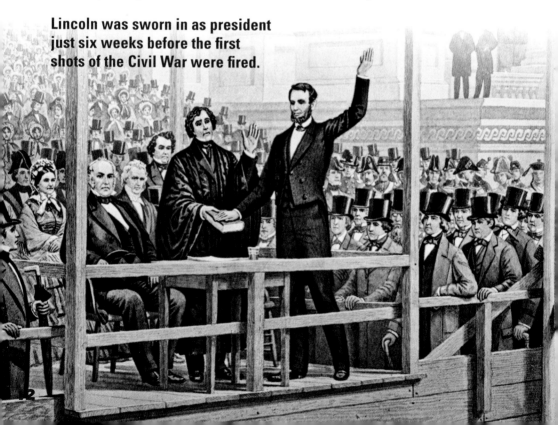

Lincoln was sworn in as president just six weeks before the first shots of the Civil War were fired.

Before Lincoln even took office, however, the country began to crumble. On December 20, 1860, South Carolina became the first state to secede from the Union. By February 1, 1861, six more Southern states had seceded. Three days later, the seven states joined together to form a new country called the Confederate States of America. Former U.S. senator and secretary of war Jefferson Davis was elected the new nation's president.

Lincoln was dismayed at this development. "We must settle this question now," he said, "whether in a free government the minority have the right to break up the government whenever they choose." He believed that the secession threatened the democratic ideals that the nation had been founded on. If the Union fell apart, Lincoln feared it would "prove the incapability of the people to govern themselves."

When he took office on March 4, Lincoln spoke of the inability of secession to break apart the Union. He claimed that it was not legally possible for a state to leave the nation and that the Confederate states were still a part of the United States. He proposed that differences between the two groups be solved peacefully and stated that the Union would not attack the Confederates unless it was attacked first. However, he also noted that he would not give up control of U.S. government properties in the South. "You can have no conflict," Lincoln said, addressing the Confederates, "without being yourselves the aggressors. . . . We are not enemies, but friends."

LINCOLN'S FIRST INAUGURAL ADDRESS

President Lincoln delivered his first inaugural address upon taking office on March 4, 1861. In it, he expressed his sadness over the recent secession of the Southern states. He also reinforced his devotion to keeping the Union whole. See page 60 for a link to view excerpts of Lincoln's handwritten draft of the speech online.

Brother Against Brother

Almost immediately after taking up his duties as president, Lincoln received word that Union troops at Fort Sumter, located off the coast of South Carolina, needed food and other supplies. Many of his advisers argued that sending the supplies would anger Confederates. The fort was located in Confederate territory, and keeping the fort defended could be taken as an act of Union aggression. However, by not sending the supplies, the Union—and its new president—would appear weak.

Jefferson Davis was the first and only president of the Confederate States of America.

Fort Sumter was named after General Thomas Sumter, a hero of the Revolutionary War.

Lincoln refused to give in to his advisers. He notified the governor of South Carolina that he would be sending supplies to the men at Fort Sumter, promising that no weapons or ammunition would be included in the delivery. In response, the Confederates demanded that Fort Sumter be evacuated. When their demand was refused, the Confederate army began firing cannons at the fort. The Civil War had begun.

Though it pained him to fight against states he still considered part of his country, Lincoln could not allow the Confederate attack on Fort Sumter to go unanswered. Doing so would in effect recognize their

More than 29,000 men were killed in the Battle of Chancellorsville, in Virginia.

independence. He brought the country's military leaders together and began working on a plan to take back the seceded states by force. Lincoln believed that the conflict would end quickly, but he was soon proven wrong.

The North's goal was to completely take over the South, winning control of major cities, waterways, and military outposts. The South, on the other hand, had only to defend its territory. It had no desire to take land from the Union. It simply wanted to establish itself as an independent nation. As a result, the North had the more difficult path to victory.

Invading the North

By 1863, the war was still raging on, with neither side in a winning position. In early May, Confederate general Robert E. Lee and his Army of Northern Virginia defeated Union general Joseph Hooker's Army of the Potomac at the Battle of Chancellorsville in Virginia. At the same time, Union forces in the west were making progress as they moved south into Confederate territory along the Mississippi River.

Before his home state of Virginia left the Union, Robert E. Lee opposed secession. However, he eventually chose to support his state's decision.

A VIEW FROM ABROAD

Throughout the Civil War, the Confederacy sought support from foreign nations. Approval from countries such as France and Great Britain would strengthen the case for Southern independence.

Southern cotton and tobacco exports had historically given the slave states a strong economic link to Europe, but a Union naval blockade along the Confederate coastline stood in the way of trade during the war. Ending the war would allow trade to resume. In addition, leaders such as British prime minister Henry John Temple and French emperor Napoleon III both personally supported Confederate goals. However, both leaders determined that opposing the Union would be a poor choice, and no foreign countries ever entered the Civil War.

Inspired by his victory at Chancellorsville, Lee hatched a plan to invade the Union. His idea was to move north along the Shenandoah valley in the east, forcing the Union to move more troops and other resources out of the Mississippi valley to defend their territory to the east. Lee also hoped that by attacking Union territory and demonstrating the Confederates' strength, he would diminish Northern support for the war and help persuade foreign allies to aid the Confederacy.

Lee began marching his troops north toward

General George G. Meade (above) had more than 20 years of military experience when President Lincoln chose him as General Joseph Hooker's replacement.

Pennsylvania. He expected to encounter General Hooker and the Army of the Potomac again, and he was confident that he would win once more.

Three Bloody Days

General Lee and an army of 75,000 men arrived in Pennsylvania in June. As troops approached the town of Gettysburg, they were surprised to find that the Army of the Potomac was drawing near—earlier than Lee had expected. He was also surprised to learn that General Hooker was no longer leading the Union forces. President Lincoln had replaced Hooker with General George G. Meade on June 28.

General George Pickett led around 15,000 Confederate soldiers in a charge that turned out to be a major strategic error for the Confederates.

On June 30, the first Union forces arrived in Gettysburg, where Meade hoped to meet Lee's army and stop it from progressing any farther into the North. The following morning, shots were fired when a party of Confederates looking for supplies entered Gettysburg and encountered Union soldiers. Over the course of the day, the battle grew and moved toward the outskirts of town. By the evening, Union troops had been forced out of positions to the west of Gettysburg and retreated to high ground at Cemetery Ridge, just outside of town. There, they used the advantage of being on higher ground to hold off Confederate troops until it grew too dark to fight. Both the Union and Confederate forces had suffered thousands of **casualties**.

Combat resumed the next morning. Tens of thousands more men on each side fought and died that day. The Union was able to hold its position on Cemetery Ridge, despite suffering heavy losses.

General Lee knew that if the battle lasted too long his troops would eventually run out of supplies, because they were far from home territory. In an effort to finally end the battle, he decided to launch a strong assault on Cemetery Ridge on the morning of July 3. The attack began with heavy cannon fire, which failed to do significant damage to the Union forces high up on the ridge. Lee then commanded a large portion of his men to charge 1 mile (1.6 kilometers) across an open field toward the ridge. This attack later became known as Pickett's Charge, named for General George Pickett, who helped lead the charge. As the Confederates rushed toward the ridge, the Union troops fired on them. More than half of the charging Confederates were killed, many others were injured, and the attack was a failure. At this point, Lee knew his army was defeated. The general and his army began retreating south toward Virginia on July 4. After the devastating loss at Gettysburg, the South would never again make an attack on Union soil.

CHAPTER 2

PAYING TRIBUTE

Bodies littered the fields of Gettysburg in the aftermath of the battle.

THE BATTLE OF GETTYSBURG

took a heavy toll on both sides. Around 3,100 Northern troops and 4,500 Southern troops were killed during the three days of bloody combat. Around 50,000 others were either missing or wounded. With the war in high gear, neither side had the time or the resources to tend to the dead bodies strewn across the battlefield on the outskirts of Gettysburg.

Governor Andrew Curtin witnessed horrible sights as he toured the Gettysburg battlefield.

The Governor at Gettysburg

Soon after the battle's conclusion, Pennsylvania governor Andrew Curtin arrived in Gettysburg to survey the damage that had been done to the town, its residents, and the surrounding area. Curtin visited with the sick and wounded soldiers who had been left behind to recover, and walked through the nearby battlefield. There, where thousands of men had clashed just days earlier, he saw corpses that had been hastily buried in shallow graves and mangled bodies left lying where they had fallen.

The governor was deeply affected by the sight. He knew that the exposed bodies would soon decay. Those bodies that had been buried in the fields would be plowed over when farmers began preparing to plant their crops, and homemade grave markers would be washed away by rain. Curtin decided that something should be done to make sure the bodies of the dead Union soldiers were treated respectfully and buried in proper graves.

Curtin's duties as governor prevented him from spending too much time in Gettysburg. He had to return to the capital city of Harrisburg. Before doing so, he

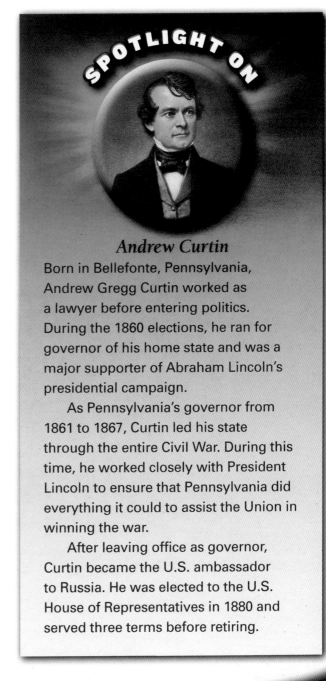

SPOTLIGHT ON

Andrew Curtin

Born in Bellefonte, Pennsylvania, Andrew Gregg Curtin worked as a lawyer before entering politics. During the 1860 elections, he ran for governor of his home state and was a major supporter of Abraham Lincoln's presidential campaign.

As Pennsylvania's governor from 1861 to 1867, Curtin led his state through the entire Civil War. During this time, he worked closely with President Lincoln to ensure that Pennsylvania did everything it could to assist the Union in winning the war.

After leaving office as governor, Curtin became the U.S. ambassador to Russia. He was elected to the U.S. House of Representatives in 1880 and served three terms before retiring.

appointed local attorney David Wills to oversee the planning and creation of a cemetery to honor the men who had died in the Battle of Gettysburg.

Planning the Cemetery

Wills invited other local residents to form the Gettysburg Cemetery Commission and immediately began designing the cemetery. The commission eventually settled on a semicircular design that grouped graves together according to the home states of the deceased. At the central point of the semicircle would be a **monument**.

Governor Curtin wanted the cemetery to be a fitting tribute to the soldiers who had died at the Battle of Gettysburg. This photo shows Cemetery Hill in the distance and land that was part of the Gettysburg battlefield in the foreground.

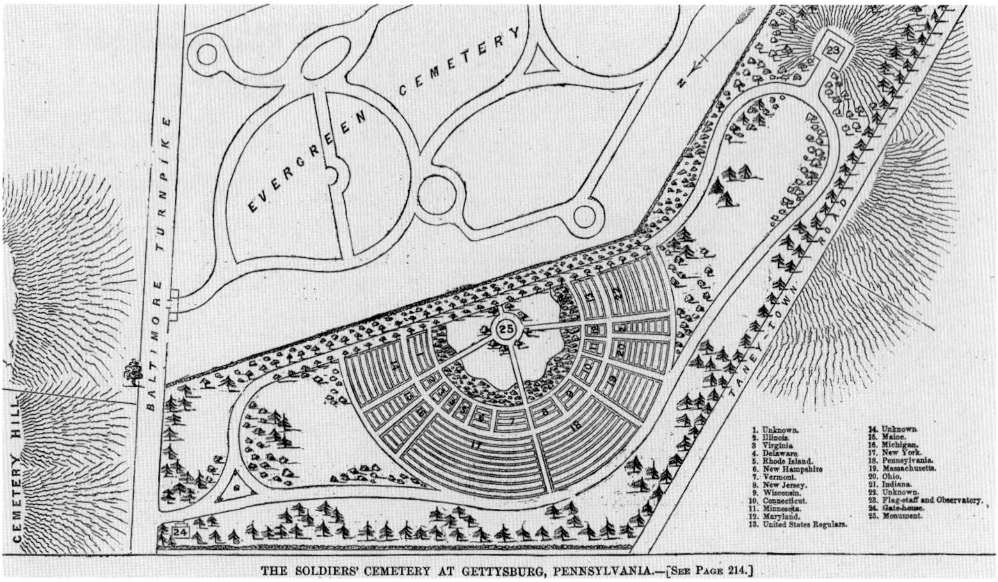
EVERGREEN CEMETERY
BALTIMORE TURNPIKE
CEMETERY HILL
TANEY-TOWN ROAD
1. Unknown.
2. Illinois.
3 Virginia
4. Delaware
5. Rhode Island.
6. New Hampshire
7. Vermont.
8. New Jersey.
9. Wisconsin.
10. Connecticut.
11. Minnesota.
12. Maryland.
13. United States Regulars.
14. Unknown
15. Maine.
16. Michigan.
17. New York.
18. Pennsylvania.
19. Massachusetts.
20. Ohio.
21. Indiana.
22. Unknown.
23. Flag-staff and Observatory.
24. Gate-house.
25. Monument.
THE SOLDIERS' CEMETERY AT GETTYSBURG, PENNSYLVANIA.—[See Page 214.]

David Wills prepared a careful plan of the proposed cemetery.

Smaller states were located closer to the monument, while larger states were arranged toward the outside of the semicircle. There was also a space designated for the graves of unidentified bodies.

Wills submitted this plan to Governor Curtin on July 24. Curtin immediately approved it and put Wills in contact with the governors of the other Union states represented in the cemetery. They all approved the design as well, allowing Wills to move ahead with the cemetery's construction. He found a suitable 17-acre (7-hectare) parcel of land on the Gettysburg battlefield and purchased it on behalf of the state of Pennsylvania. Several other states contributed funds to pay for the collection and burial of the bodies, as well as for the cemetery's landscaping and construction.

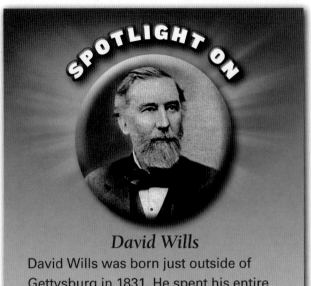

David Wills

David Wills was born just outside of Gettysburg in 1831. He spent his entire life in the area and attended the nearby Pennsylvania College, where he trained to become an attorney. After graduating, Wills practiced law and led the county's school district.

Wills and his family witnessed the Battle of Gettysburg firsthand. They sheltered neighbors in their cellar as soldiers fought in the streets just outside. After the battle, Wills played a major role in helping the town recover. He took part in gathering and distributing supplies to aid the wounded and fought to secure government compensation for the farmers whose fields were ruined by the combat.

The Guest List

As progress continued on the cemetery, Wills began preparing a dedication ceremony that would pay tribute to the fallen soldiers' sacrifice. He decided on the date of October 23 and asked politician and noted public speaker Edward Everett to prepare a speech for the event. Everett wrote back soon, informing Wills that he had a very busy speaking schedule and would not have enough time to write a fitting speech by October 23. He wanted to ensure that the ceremony was marked by a speech that was truly worthy of the event. "The occasion is one of great importance," Everett wrote, "not to be dismissed with a few sentimental or patriotic commonplaces."

As a result, Wills agreed to push back the date of the ceremony to November 19. With the event scheduled, he wrote letters inviting a variety of public figures, including members of Congress and military leaders such as George Meade and Winfield Scott. He also extended an invitation to President Lincoln. Though Everett was scheduled as the ceremony's main speaker, Wills thought it would be fitting if Lincoln were given time for a brief statement. In his invitation, he asked Lincoln to "set apart these grounds for their sacred use by a few appropriate remarks."

General Winfield Scott ran for president in 1852, but was defeated by Franklin Pierce.

In his preparations for the cemetery and its dedication ceremony, David Wills corresponded often with Governor Curtin, Edward Everett, and many other important leaders. See page 60 for a link to read several of Wills's letters online.

The Right Words

President Lincoln accepted Wills's invitation and began thinking about what he would like to say at the ceremony. In the days leading up to the event, he thought carefully about the battle, the war, and his feelings about the country's division. The victory at Gettysburg had given him an optimistic view of the Union's chances of winning. Lincoln decided to use his speech to help spread these feelings of optimism. He hoped to both honor the fallen soldiers and encourage the surviving troops to continue fighting.

President Lincoln carefully prepared his remarks for the cemetery's dedication.

The Battle of Vicksburg, Mississippi, ended on July 4, 1863, when Confederate general John C. Pemberton surrendered to Union general Ulysses S. Grant.

The Union victory at Gettysburg occurred on July 4, with Lee's retreat. This same day the Union had another major win, at the Battle of Vicksburg in Mississippi. July 4 was also the anniversary of the Declaration of Independence, the document that first marked the United States as a free nation. This connection may have led Lincoln to think about the connections between the country's founding principles and its current situation.

Little is known of Lincoln's exact process for writing his speech. However, it is very likely that he began working on at least an outline before leaving Washington for Pennsylvania. He may even have prepared an entire draft. Some historians believe that Lincoln began writing the speech in Washington, and then discussed his ideas for finishing it with Secretary of State William H. Seward as they traveled by train to Pennsylvania for the ceremony.

Lincoln's Arrival

President Lincoln arrived in Gettysburg on the afternoon of November 18. That evening, he attended a welcoming gathering along with other important guests. Secretary of State Seward delivered a speech. Seward spoke out against slavery and discussed the importance of bringing the country back together. He said that he "saw, 40 years ago, that slavery was opening before this people a graveyard,

William H. Seward served as U.S. secretary of state from 1861 to 1869.

David Wills's house stands today as a popular tourist destination.

that was to be filled with brothers falling in mutual political combat." He also noted that he wished the North and South had been able to settle their differences peacefully and that he hoped the war would soon end with a reunited country.

Meanwhile, Lincoln continued to plan for the following day's speech. As the evening's festivities wound down, he went to David Wills's home, where he was to spend the night. It was there that he is believed to have put the finishing touches on his speech.

CHAPTER 3

OF THE PEOPLE, BY THE PEOPLE, FOR THE PEOPLE

A huge crowd gathered to watch the dedication ceremony.

ON THE MORNING OF November 19, a crowd of around 15,000 people gathered in the cool fall weather to witness the dedication of the Gettysburg National Cemetery. People surrounded a small stage that had been constructed for the event. Local citizens, government officials, members of the press, and foreign **diplomats** were all present. Union soldiers who had fought and been injured in the Battle of Gettysburg were also part of the large crowd gathered there to watch the ceremony.

This photograph was taken shortly before President Lincoln passed by on horseback on his way to the ceremony.

The Procession

At around 9:00 a.m., a military **procession** formed in the center of Gettysburg. An hour later, it began moving toward the cemetery grounds. Behind the procession rode President Lincoln, Everett, and a variety of government officials from across the Union. Spectators watched as the procession made its way into the cemetery, accompanied by a musical performance by Birgfield's Band of Philadelphia, Pennsylvania. The members of the military reached their designated positions and saluted as the president rode past on horseback.

Once the procession was complete and everyone was in place, the event began. The Reverend Thomas Hewlings Stockton, chaplain of the U.S. House of Representatives, opened the ceremony with a short prayer. Afterward, the Marine Band gave a short musical performance, and then Edward Everett took the stage.

Everett's Speech

Everett had long held a reputation as one of the nation's greatest **orators**. His fame was all it took to draw a huge crowd, and he spoke often at events throughout the country. As a result, many of the people at the cemetery that day had gathered to hear Everett, rather than Lincoln.

Everett lived up to his reputation that day. He spoke for more than two hours, delivering his entire speech from memory, with no notes

Prior to the outbreak of the Civil War, Edward Everett spoke out in favor of finding compromise between the North and the South.

or other aids. The huge crowd listened carefully to his every word as he unfolded a dramatic retelling of the battle that had taken place just months earlier, right where they were standing. Everett had spent weeks researching reports of the battle, and he hoped to bring it to life for his listeners in perfect detail.

He began his speech with an extended comparison between the Battle of Gettysburg and great military victories of the ancient Greeks. He also included a description of traditional burial methods used in ancient Greece. Everett spoke out against the Confederacy, painting it as an enemy of American values and freedom. He referred to secession as a "crime" and glorified the heroic deeds of the Union army. Many people in the

Everett spoke in great detail about the Battle of Gettysburg.

audience were moved to tears by his stunning performance at the podium.

Lincoln at Last

After Everett's speech, an orchestra performed a hymn composed especially for the occasion by Benjamin Brown French, the U.S. commissioner for public buildings. Once the orchestra was finished playing, President Lincoln approached the podium. He wore a black suit, white gloves, and a tall silk hat with a black band wrapped around it to indicate mourning.

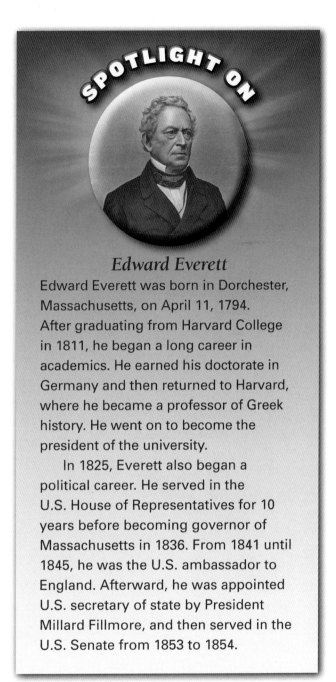

SPOTLIGHT ON

Edward Everett

Edward Everett was born in Dorchester, Massachusetts, on April 11, 1794. After graduating from Harvard College in 1811, he began a long career in academics. He earned his doctorate in Germany and then returned to Harvard, where he became a professor of Greek history. He went on to become the president of the university.

In 1825, Everett also began a political career. He served in the U.S. House of Representatives for 10 years before becoming governor of Massachusetts in 1836. From 1841 until 1845, he was the U.S. ambassador to England. Afterward, he was appointed U.S. secretary of state by President Millard Fillmore, and then served in the U.S. Senate from 1853 to 1854.

Lincoln wore the band not just in honor of the troops who died at Gettysburg, but also for his young son Willie, who had died the year before.

THE DIARY OF BENJAMIN BROWN FRENCH

Benjamin Brown French was a strong supporter of President Lincoln and the effort to end slavery. In a diary entry from the day of the Gettysburg Address, Brown writes of Lincoln's speech and recalls the nation's long struggle with slavery. See page 60 for a link to see the original diary pages online.

Lincoln's tall, lanky body and high-pitched voice made him a strange figure at the podium. However, in the course of just two minutes, he made a more powerful argument for the preservation of the Union than Everett had managed in two hours. Fewer than 300 words long, the president's speech was direct and to the point.

The huge crowd paid close attention to President Lincoln's every word.

Lincoln's speech was short, but powerful.

The Gettysburg Address

Four score and seven years ago our fathers brought forth on this continent, a new nation, conceived in liberty, and dedicated to the proposition that "all men are created equal." Now we are engaged in a great civil war, testing whether that nation, or any nation so conceived, and so dedicated, can long endure. We are met on a great battlefield of that war. We have come to dedicate a portion of that field, as a final resting place for those who here gave their lives that that nation might live. It is altogether fitting and proper that we should do this. But, in a larger sense, we cannot dedicate—we cannot consecrate—we cannot hallow—this ground. The brave men, living and dead, who struggled here, have consecrated it, far above our poor power to add or detract. The world will little note, nor

YESTERDAY'S HEADLINES

On February 20, 1862, with the Civil War in full swing, President Lincoln's 11-year-old son, Willie, died of typhoid fever. During the boy's sickness, Lincoln worked hard to keep his worries about his son hidden as he went about guiding the country through one of its most difficult times.

Lincoln mourned openly when Willie finally passed away, and people were amazed at the president's ability to cope with such a horrible situation. Writer Nathaniel Parker Willis described Lincoln at his son's funeral: "There sat the man, with a burden on his brain at which the world marvels—bent now with the load at both heart and brain." Despite his sadness, Lincoln continued to provide strong leadership to the Union as the war went on.

long remember, what we say here, but it can never forget what they did here. It is for us the living, rather, to be dedicated here to the unfinished work which they who fought here have thus far so nobly advanced. It is rather for us to be here dedicated to the great task remaining before us— that from these honored dead we take increased devotion to that cause for which they gave the last full measure of devotion—that we here highly resolve that these dead shall not have died in vain—that this nation, under God, shall have a new birth of freedom— and that government of the people, by the people, for the people, shall not perish from the earth.

History in the Making

The audience was stunned as Lincoln made his way back to his seat. The two-minute speech was far shorter than most speeches of the day, and it took several moments for the audience to understand that the speech was over. A choir performed one last piece of music before the day's final speaker, the Reverend Henry Lewis Baugher of Gettysburg, took the stage. Dr. Baugher offered a closing prayer, and the ceremony was over. Though the event had lasted several hours and the audience had heard from several speakers, it was Lincoln's words that would mark November 19, 1863, as a historic day.

Lincoln's well-chosen words touched the emotions of the audience.

CHAPTER 4

TIMELESS WORDS

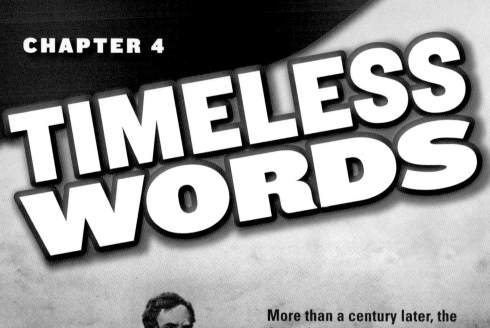

More than a century later, the Gettysburg Address remains one of the best-known speeches ever delivered.

DURING HIS SPEECH, PRESIDENT
Lincoln stated that "the world will little note, nor
long remember, what we say here." He believed
that while the sacrifices made by the soldiers
in the Battle of Gettysburg would live on as
an important part of history, the dedication of
the cemetery was a minor event that would be
forgotten by most people. While Lincoln was right
that people would long remember the battle itself,
he greatly underestimated the impact his words
would have.

Reactions

Immediately after delivering his address and returning to his seat, Lincoln is reported to have told a nearby bodyguard that the speech had been "a flat failure and the people are disappointed." This negative portrayal of the speech is far from accurate. Witnesses to the event, such as hymn composer Benjamin French, reported that the crowd met Lincoln's words with approval. Even Edward Everett was impressed with Lincoln's ability to say so much with so few words. In a letter to Lincoln soon after the speech, he wrote, "I should be glad, if I could flatter myself that I came as near to the central idea of the occasion, in two hours, as you did in two minutes."

LINCOLN'S GETTYSBURG ADDRESS
Abraham Lincoln delivered his Gettysburg Address on this spot Nov. 19, 1863, when the Soldiers' National Cemetery was dedicated. This monument, a memorial to the soldiers who fell here, was the first one erected on the battlefield. The corner statues represent War, History, Peace, and Plenty, with the Genius of Liberty surmounting the column.
Dedicated July 1, 1869
Architect, J. G. Batterson
Sculptor, Randolph Rogers

Today, a memorial marks the spot where Lincoln delivered the address.

The words of both Lincoln and Everett were reported on and printed in newspapers across the country in the following days. Such articles reflected more on the nation's divided political feelings than the actual speeches. Newspapers that supported Lincoln's policies praised his words, while those that opposed him dismissed the speech as insignificant.

What It Meant

The Gettysburg Address is as notable for what Lincoln did not say as for what he did say. In his two minutes at the podium, Lincoln did not mention slavery, the

YESTERDAY'S HEADLINES

Reactions to Lincoln's Gettysburg Address varied among the country's many newspapers. To read one report, it might seem as if Lincoln had delivered the finest speech the nation had ever heard. To read another, it would appear he had made a fool of himself. For example, the *Chicago Tribune* reported that "the dedicatory remarks by President Lincoln will live among the annals of man." In the very same city, the *Chicago Times* expressed a very different interpretation of the speech. The paper's article on the dedication read, "The cheeks of every American must tingle with shame as he reads the silly, flat, and dishwatery utterances."

TODAY'S PERSPECTIVE

Today, the Gettysburg Address is one of the most well-known and respected speeches in American history. For most Americans, the words "Four score and seven years ago" immediately call to mind an image of Lincoln at the podium. Modern speakers continue to study the address as an example for their own work.

Lincoln's words are inscribed in stone at the Lincoln Memorial in Washington, D.C., and original handwritten copies of the speech are on display at several locations. Each year, millions of people travel to see the president's words, which stand as one of the defining documents of American history.

Confederacy, or the Union. Unlike Everett, he did not recount details of the Battle of Gettysburg or speak out against the South. Instead, he spoke in broad terms about ending the war and bringing the country back together. He lamented the loss of so many men in combat, but referred to the war as "unfinished work."

Lincoln's speech portrayed the Civil War as a fight to mend a broken nation. It also highlighted how important it was to remember this fight and what it stood for: the strength of democracy and the freedoms that go along with it.

This crowd shot is the only known photograph of Lincoln at Gettysburg.

Preserving the Speech

At the time of the Gettysburg Address, the technology for recording sound and video had not yet been invented. Cameras existed, and a photographer was present at the event. There is at least one photo of Lincoln at the ceremony, but there are no known photos of him giving his speech. After Everett finished speaking, the photographer began setting up to take pictures of Lincoln. However, the Gettysburg Address was so short that he was still setting up his equipment by the time Lincoln was done.

To piece together a picture of the president's delivery and his inspirational words, we rely on eyewitness accounts and Lincoln's handwritten drafts. Today, there are five known copies of the speech. Two were written near the time of the speech and given by Lincoln to his private secretaries. Lincoln wrote the other three copies many days after giving the speech. One was a gift to Edward Everett. The other two were given to historians who had requested them. Since then, these drafts have been carefully preserved as historic documents.

Lincoln's handwritten drafts of the speech can be viewed at several museums.

Executive Mansion,

Washington, _____ , 186 .

Four score and seven years ago our fathers brought forth, upon this continent, a new nation, conceived in liberty, and dedicated to the proposition that "all men are created equal"

Now we are engaged in a great civil war, testing whether that nation, or any nation so conceived, and so dedicated, can long endure. We are met on a great battle field of that war. We have come to dedicate a portion of it, as a final resting place for those who died here, that the nation might live. This we may, in all propriety do. But, in a larger sense, we can not dedicate — we can not — hallow this ground —

A Lasting Legacy

In the years following the Gettysburg Address, the speech's reputation grew more positive. In 1868, the *New York Times* referred to it as "President Lincoln's celebrated Gettysburg Address." Three years later, the popular journalist Horace Greeley wrote, "I doubt that our national literature contains a finer gem than that little speech at the Gettysburg celebration." Massachusetts senator Charles Sumner even claimed, "The battle itself was less important than the speech." He wisely and accurately wrote, "The world at once noted what he said, and will never cease to remember it."

Horace Greeley founded a newspaper called the *New York Tribune* in 1841.

A FIRSTHAND LOOK AT
THE GETTYSBURG ADDRESS

Five handwritten drafts of the Gettysburg Address are known to exist today. These documents were written by President Lincoln himself and have been carefully preserved. Lincoln gave one to his secretary John Nicolay. See page 60 for a link to view a part of this document online.

MAP OF THE EVENTS

What Happened Where?

Steinwehr Avenue

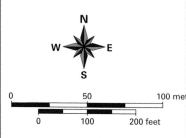

New York

Ohio

Pennsylvania

Gettysburg ●

New
Jersey

Maryland

West
Virginia

Washington, DC ●

Delaware

Virginia

N

W ✦ E

S

| 0 | | 50 | | 100 met |

| 0 | | 100 | | 200 feet |

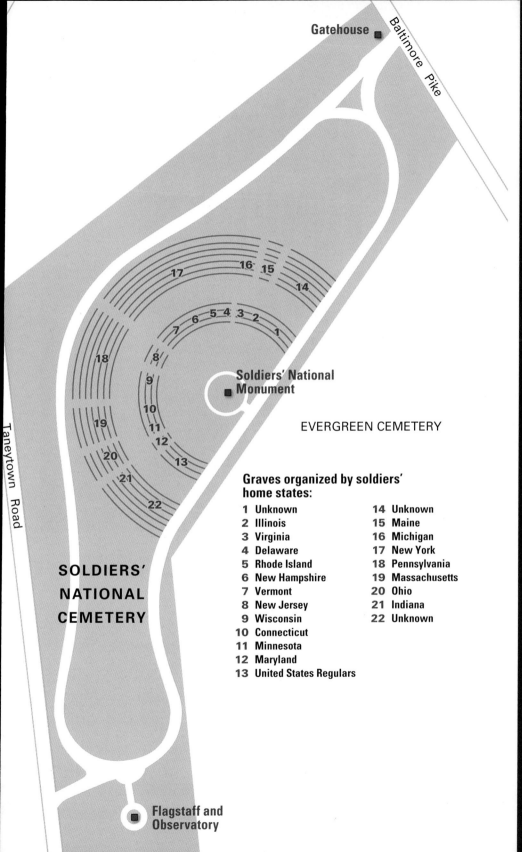

Gatehouse

Baltimore Pike

17 16 15 14

6 5 4 3 2
7 1

18

8

9

Soldiers' National
Monument

EVERGREEN CEMETERY

10

19

11

12

20

13

21

22

Taneytown Road

SOLDIERS'
NATIONAL
CEMETERY

**Graves organized by soldiers'
home states:**

1 Unknown
2 Illinois
3 Virginia
4 Delaware
5 Rhode Island
6 New Hampshire
7 Vermont
8 New Jersey
9 Wisconsin
10 Connecticut
11 Minnesota
12 Maryland
13 United States Regulars

14 Unknown
15 Maine
16 Michigan
17 New York
18 Pennsylvania
19 Massachusetts
20 Ohio
21 Indiana
22 Unknown

Flagstaff and
Observatory

A Nation Reunited

The site at Appomattox Court House where Lee surrendered to Grant became a national historical monument in 1940.

In the months following Gettysburg, the Union military began to gain momentum in its fight against the Confederacy. Finally, on April 9, 1865, Confederate general Robert E. Lee surrendered to Union general Ulysses S. Grant at Appomattox Court House in Virginia. The war was essentially over.

JOHN WILKES BOOTH WAS A WELL-KNOWN

Five days later, President Lincoln was shot while attending a play at Ford's Theatre in Washington, D.C. He died the next day. His killer, John Wilkes Booth, was a supporter of slavery who was angered by the Confederacy's defeat. Though the Union was reunited, it would take many years to heal the differences between the North and the South.

John Wilkes Booth shot President Lincoln in the back of the head.

ACTOR BEFORE HE KILLED LINCOLN.

INFLUENTIAL INDIVIDUALS

Abraham Lincoln

Edward Everett (1794–1865) was a noted public speaker. He spoke for more than two hours before President Lincoln delivered the Gettysburg Address.

Robert E. Lee (1807–1870) was a general in the Confederate army. His defeat at the Battle of Gettysburg marked the beginning of the end for the Confederacy.

Abraham Lincoln (1809–1865) was the 16th president of the United States. His leadership during the Civil War helped to reunite the country.

George G. Meade (1815–1872) was a Union general during the Civil War. He led the Army of the Potomac to victory at the Battle of Gettysburg.

Andrew Curtin (1817–1894) was the governor of Pennsylvania during the Civil War. After witnessing the aftermath of the Battle of Gettysburg, he called for the construction of a cemetery to honor the fallen soldiers.

David Wills (1831–1894) was a Gettysburg attorney who led the planning of the Gettysburg National Cemetery.

George G. Meade

David Wills

TIMELINE

1776

July 4
The Continental Congress adopts the Declaration of Independence.

1858

Abraham Lincoln rises to national attention as a result of his debates with Congressman Stephen A. Douglas.

1861

February 4
The Confederate States of America is established.

March 4
Lincoln takes office.

April 12
Fort Sumter is attacked, marking the beginning of the Civil War.

1860

November 6
Lincoln is elected president.

December 20
South Carolina becomes the first state to secede from the Union.

1863

July 1-3
Union forces led by General George G. Meade defeat Confederate forces led by General Robert E. Lee at the Battle of Gettysburg.

November 19
President Lincoln delivers the Gettysburg Address.

1865

April 9
General Lee surrenders at Appomattox Court House, bringing the Civil War to a close.

April 14
Lincoln is shot by John Wilkes Booth and dies the next morning.

LIVING HISTORY

Primary sources provide firsthand evidence about a topic. Witnesses to a historical event create primary sources. They include autobiographies, newspaper reports of the time, oral histories, photographs, and memoirs. A secondary source analyzes primary sources and is one step or more removed from the event. Secondary sources include textbooks, encyclopedias, and commentaries. To view the following primary and secondary sources, go to www.factsfornow.scholastic.com. Enter the keywords **Gettysburg Address** and look for the Living History logo Σ¡.

Σ¡ The Diary of Benjamin Brown French Benjamin Brown French was the U.S. commissioner for public buildings at the time of the Gettysburg Address. He composed a hymn that was performed at the opening of the Gettysburg National Cemetery. His diary includes an account of Lincoln's speech and the audience's reaction.

Σ¡ The Gettysburg Address Five handwritten copies of President Lincoln's Gettysburg Address exist today. One is located at Cornell University, one is at the Illinois State Historical Library, one is at the Lincoln Room of the White House, and two are at the Library of Congress. Excerpts from one of the Library of Congress's copies are available online.

Σ¡ The Letters of David Wills During his planning of the Gettysburg National Cemetery and its opening ceremony, David Wills corresponded with many important leaders. Much of this correspondence was preserved and is available to read online.

Σ¡ Lincoln's First Inaugural Address Upon taking office in March 1861, President Lincoln stated the importance of reuniting the country. Excerpts from Lincoln's handwritten draft of the inaugural speech are available online from the Library of Congress.

RESOURCES

Books

Benoit, Peter. *Abraham Lincoln*. New York: Children's Press, 2012.
Benoit, Peter. *The Civil War*. New York: Children's Press, 2012.
Gregory, Josh. *Gettysburg*. New York: Children's Press, 2012.

**Visit this Scholastic Web site for
more information on the Gettysburg Address:
www.factsfornow.scholastic.com
Enter the keywords Gettysburg Address**

GLOSSARY

abolition (a-buh-LIH-shuhn) the official end of something

casualties (KAZH-oo-uhl-teez) people killed or wounded during warfare

diplomats (DIP-luh-mats) people whose job is to officially represent their countries' governments in a foreign country

draft (DRAFT) a first version of a document, or one that is not final

economy (i-KAHN-uh-mee) the system of buying, selling, making things, and managing money in a place

industries (IN-duh-streez) manufacturing companies and other businesses

legislature (LEJ-uh-slay-chur) the part of government that is responsible for making and changing laws

monument (MAHN-yuh-muhnt) a statue, building, or other structure that reminds people of an event or a person

orators (OR-uh-turz) public speakers

procession (pruh-SESH-uhn) a number of people walking or driving along a route in an orderly way as part of a public festival, a religious service, or a parade

secede (si-SEED) to formally withdraw from a group

unanimous (yoo-NAN-uh-muhss) with everyone in agreement

INDEX

Page numbers in *italics* indicate illustrations.

ABOUT THE AUTHOR

Josh Gregory writes and edits books for kids. He lives in Chicago, Illinois.